THE HUSBAND GAMBLE

THE WEDDING WAGER

BOOK THIRTEEN

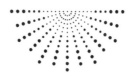

JUDE KNIGHT

THE WEDDING WAGER

TITCHFIELD
PRESS

THE HUSBAND GAMBLE

When the pawn becomes Queen, she and the opposing King will both win the game of love

Amaryllis Fernhill fled her wedding to her uncle's thrice-widowed crony, ruining herself in the eyes of ton. Three years on, she needs a husband to unlock her inheritance—preferably one who wants little to do with the society that has rejected her. Can a countess famous for making unlikely matches make one for her?

The Earl of Hythe needs a countess who will add luster to his family name and support his career as a diplomat and politician in London and the capitals of Europe. But he also wants a wife, a partner, a friend. No one he meets seeks to know the man behind the title. Can the matchmaking countess succeed in finding a perfect lady with a caring heart?

Rilla and Hythe write one another off as all wrong, but when they are drawn together over a chess board at the countess's house party, they discover how right such a match could be.

CHAPTER ONE

In the village of Pluffington-on-Memmerbeck, Amaryllis Fernhill's wedding is one of the high points of the past fifty years—a wonderful spectacle, and one in which the villagers' betters were bested. Even better than the time the great-grandfather of the current earl set his horse cavorting in front of the blacksmith's daughter and was bucked off into the duck pond.

The little ones, who were not present for the wedding, beg for the story when night draws in and the fire sinks low and bedtime beckons. "Please, Granny (or Gaffer, as the case may be), tell us the story of the stolen bride?"

["The Abduction of Amaryllis Fernhill", in *Collected Tales from the Villages of England*, by a Gentleman]

The first hurdle was over. Lady Octavia Sewell had agreed to receive them despite the black mark hanging over Amaryllis Fernhill's reputation. Rilla pasted on an expression of confidence, took Cousin Felicia's arm, and followed the butler up the stairs.

Rilla had underestimated the challenges she would face in meeting the terms of her father's will. She was no beauty, and her reputation had been shredded three years ago. On the other hand, in those three years she had learned to dress to enhance the assets she did have. She couldn't do much about her reputation, but the worst of the allegations were untrue and, after all, a five-thousand-pound dowry was not to be sneered at.

Apparently, the dowry was not enough to attract the kind of suitor she was willing to consider. Not when she was the famous Amaryllis Fernhill, the woman who had been abducted from the altar three years ago, and who had seemingly disappeared off the face of the earth until part way through this year's London Season. Suddenly, there she was, her companion an elderly and distant cousin, ready to enter the marriage mart.

The Season had been a disaster. The summer and autumn at different spa towns, and the succession of events to which Cousin Felicia managed to garner an invitation, a complete waste of time. She collected plenty of the wrong kind of suitor as well as snubs from those who thought they knew precisely what she had been up to for the last few years. But not one respectable gentleman she trusted enough to grant him her future.

Rilla had no intention of being left worse off after marriage than before.

They had arrived. The butler opened the door and announced them. "Miss Amaryllis Fernhill. Lady Felicia Barker."

Amaryllis could not help another sigh of relief when Lady Sewell rose to greet Cousin Felicia with enthusiasm. "My dear Lady Barker! I am delighted to see you! I had no idea you were in the area."

"We travelled here to see you, Lady Sewell." Cousin Felicia's straightforward approach was a great delight to Rilla, not least because of the poisonous subtlety employed by the haut ton. She only hoped it would serve her now. "Allow me to present my cousin, Miss Amaryllis Fernhill. I believe you may be in a position to help her."

Lady Sewell turned to Rilla, and Rilla curtseyed. "Good day, Miss Fernhill."

"My lady."

Lady Sewell waved to a pair of chairs close to the sofa where she had been lounging. "Please, be seated. I have ordered refreshments." She waited until Rilla and Cousin Felicia were seated before commenting, "So you are the girl who was taken away by the fairies. And now you are back from wherever you really went and you want a husband."

Rilla decided to meet bluntness with bluntness. "If rumour is correct, my lady, I am just what you are looking for. A lady for whom your cousin Lady Osbourne will find it impossible to make a match, thus winning the wager between you. I am just desperate enough to gamble she will surprise us both, for I have tried for months, and am certainly not going to find a husband on my own."

Lady Sewell narrowed her eyes. "Are you pregnant, girl?"

Rilla supposed she had invited the question, and she managed to keep the resentment from her voice when she answered. "No, my lady. It is not possible. I am still a maiden."

"Hmm." Lady Sewell did not look pleased, but then she brightened. "But there is no way Pansy can introduce that topic into the conversation, and nor can she provide evidence if she did. It will do. It will do very well."

She smiled. "Very well, Miss Fernhill. You shall go to one of my cousin's house parties, and I shall challenge her to find you an appealing match. Let us have a cup of tea, and talk about what you are looking for in a husband."

The Earl of Hythe was already regretting his agreement to attend the party. The room he had been given was perfectly adequate. His valet Pritchard, who had been with him for years, had been busy arranging the suite of rooms while Hythe was in his bath.

Pritchard knew exactly how Hythe liked things. He had organised the dressing room and the bedside table, and had moved the chairs in the seating area so they were precisely aligned with the edge of the hearth, with the little table equidistant between the two and on the same ruler-straight line. In a dozen ways, he had removed the tiny imperfections that left Hythe unsettled.

After he was dressed again, Hythe set his travelling desk on the desk provided, and checked the desk drawers. Lady Osbourne had provided quality paper and ink. The stack of paper needed to be straightened, as did the rest of the drawer contents. That task finished, Hythe had no further excuse for lingering in his room, getting in Pritchard's way. Like it or not, he needed to go below and meet the other guests.

He blamed his sister Sophia, entirely. On second thoughts, he had opened himself to the attack. If he had never grumbled to her about the difficulty of finding a wife one could respect and even, perhaps, befriend, she would never have suggested he put himself in the hands of the acclaimed matchmaker. One who had found matches, furthermore, for people whom Society had judged unmarriageable.

Even so, Hythe would never have agreed if the marriage of his sister Felicity had not left his townhouse appallingly empty. Felicity had followed him from one diplomatic post into another, keeping house for him. His servants were perfectly competent, but they would be horrified to be asked to sit down for a chat over breakfast or of an evening.

Even Pritchard. Especially Pritchard, who was more proper than Hythe could ever be.

In addition, of course, no servant could be his hostess or be at his side during the social occasions that were so much part of his work.

"Excuse me, my lord," Pritchard said.

Hythe stepped out of his way, and Pritchard, carrying Hythe's dinner jacket as if it was the crown jewels, proceeded to lay the garment on the bed and return to the dressing room for the next item. "Dinner is at seven, my lord, with gathering in the drawing room from six thirty."

It was Pritchard's way of saying "You have at least two hours before dressing for dinner, so please go away so I can ensure anything you might choose to wear has been inspected and, if necessary, restored to a standard suitable for the Earl of Hythe."

Hythe repressed a sigh and bowed to the inevitable, though he only went as far as the passage, where he stood for a moment, his eyes shut, bracing himself to meet all those people.

It was only for a week. He could resist any plots by Lady Osbourne or her protégés for one week. *One of them might be the one for you.* He rejected the errant thought. Everyone knew that Lady Osbourne had wagered with her cousin that she could find matches for the most awkward, difficult and challenging of wallflowers and hoydens and the most unprepossessing or rascally of grooms.

Hythe knew he had little to recommend him beyond his title and his wealth. Ladies seem to prefer a man of address, who could flatter them with elegant compliments and talk for hours about frivolous matters that bored Hythe witless. Someone at ease meeting strangers and comfortable in crowds of people.

For Hythe, social occasions were an ordeal. He could manage. He had memorised a hundred different meaningless but polite responses, and practiced them in front of a mirror. He had learned which ones to trot out on which occasion.

It was not so bad if he could find a meaningful conversation in which to immerse himself, but the ladies of Society and many of the men had no interest in topics that mattered. Hythe had discovered the trick of finding a quiet corner where he could take a few deep breathes before pasting on a smile and getting back to work.

The right wife would have the skills he lacked, as his sisters did. They were both brilliant political and diplomatic hostesses, and had been happy to give their brother the benefit of their skills. Until they married. Without them, life in Society was even more exhausting than before.

He had not been able to find a bride who offered what he

needed as a man. What his title required made it even more diffi-cult. The Earl of Hythe needed a countess who could burnish the reputation of the earldom and the family. Money was irrelevant. Looks were secondary. Behaviour…

Even in his thoughts, he could not agree that behaviour was everything. Important, yes. Hythe was the head of the Belvoir family, and no stain had ever attached to their family name. His parents had been renowned for their good ton as well as their wealth, their generosity, and their wide circle of friends. His sisters were models of propriety. Felicity, his younger sister, might at times allow her vivacity to bring her to the edge of proper behaviour, but never over.

However, Hythe wanted more from marriage than a countess who could be a good hostess and who knew how to behave. Perhaps, if he had contemplated marriage a few years ago, he might have chosen one of the insipid bird brains that seemed to be the primary offering on the marriage mart. And perhaps, if he had been lucky, she might have learned to be an adequate countess.

Hythe also wanted a wife. His sisters had found love matches. So had several of his friends. He was not convinced a love match was a desirable thing—such an untidy excess of emotion did not appeal to him. In any case, he had never imagined himself in love, even when his friends were falling like flies for opera dances and Society beau-ties. He was probably not capable of the emotion.

The other kind of love he could manage very well. He had loved his parents. He held a deep and abiding affection for both of his sisters. He was sure he could be a fond and caring husband and father. All he had to do was find a wife he could talk to. It may be setting the bar too low to say a wife who did not irritate him, but that was precisely what he told Lady Osbourne when she button-holed him in Town after Sophia asked her for her help.

Someone who did not irritate him. Someone who was old enough and interesting enough to know her own mind and be prepared to have opinions and defend them. Someone who liked children and would be a good mother, for Hythe would need an heir, and hoped his son might grow up with brothers and sisters.

Someone who knew how to behave as the wife of a diplomat and a peer—that went without saying, although he said it anyway. Someone who was at ease in social situations and prepared to exercise that mastery on his behalf, though he did not put that into words, unwilling to expose his deficiencies to that extent.

He waved away Lady Osbourne's questions about appearance. Short or tall. Fair or dark. Plump or slender. What did those matter over a lifetime? "I want someone to grow old with," he told Lady Osbourne. "Should we be so blessed."

He couldn't spend the rest of the day leaning against the wall outside his room. He opened his eyes even as he took a stride down the passage, only to find his arms full of a warm fragrant female. Who gasped, and pulled backwards.

CHAPTER TWO

And Granny (or, as it might be, Gaffer) would tell what they witnessed with their own eyes, though how much the story was shaped by each onlooker, and how much it has grown with time, who can tell?

    ["The Abduction of Amaryllis Fernhill", in *Collected Tales from the Villages of England*, by a Gentleman]

Rilla sat on the window seat in the room she shared with Cousin Felicia, dreading the coming week. Would people be able to tell by looking at her where she had spent the last few years? Of course, they would not, and very few would be rude enough to ask. The artificial manners she had been taught years ago made such an open display of curiosity inappropriate for a lady.

After running away, she'd had to learn a whole new standard of what was appropriate. As artificial in its own way as those of the class she now hoped to join again, but necessary in order to fit in.

She had to at least pretend to take the social manoeuvring at this house party seriously, or it would all be for nothing.

Time to go downstairs, she told herself. Cousin Felicia had already preceded her, and would be wondering why Rilla had not followed.

Rilla's feet had become glued to the floor. Where was her courage when she needed it? Running away from the unwanted marriage her uncle planned for her had also been a gamble, but with some protections. For one thing, she trusted the friend who had helped her to escape. For another, whatever happened could hardly have been worse than marriage to an old and smelly man who only wanted her for her dowry and her prospective ability to bear him an heir. Or, the alternative future her uncle had promised if she refused.

This time, though, she could not weigh one risk against another. If she did not marry, she was doomed to a life of earning her own living, with no security and little future. Her father's will left her a dowry of five thousand pounds, but she was to receive none of it. If she married, it would go to her husband. Failing her marriage, it stayed in trust until she died, and then went to a veteran's hospital.

At least she had turned twenty-five. Now, she no longer needed her uncle's approval of her choice of groom for the dowry to be released into her husband's hands. There was the rub. Someone who would wed her, scandal and all, just to get his hands on her money might not be significantly better than poverty. It might indeed be a case of out of the frying pan into the fire.

Seeking a position as a housekeeper was definitely preferable to making a bad marriage. She would be required to manage a house either way—something she was well qualified to do. But house-keepers could resign if their employer made their life difficult.

At least this time, she would be the one to make the choice. After all, she was not obliged to marry everyone who asked. If, in fact, any one did so. No one would have the opportunity if she didn't leave her room. She took a deep breath, stepped out into the hall, turned towards the stairs, and barrelled into someone coming the other way.

"I beg your pardon," she said.

"It was my fault," replied the gentlemen. The passage was not well lit, but his eyes caught the light from a wall sconce, and beneath them she could see his grin. "I had my eyes shut," he confessed.

His candour charmed her into some of her own. "I was hurrying, because I have been hiding in my room for so long, I was afraid I was late."

He bowed. "Perhaps you will allow me to escort you? May I introduce myself, since no one else is here to perform the office? I am Hythe."

The Earl of Hythe. As a girl, she had been made to study Debrett's, though her father only permitted her the one Season, so until this year the knowledge had been entirely superfluous. He was waiting, a slight smile curving his lips. She curtseyed, delaying the moment of recognition when his eyes would glaze over and then he would give her the cut direct. "Miss Amaryllis Fernhill," she said, clearly.

It was not quite that bad, though there was no doubt he recognised her name. His bow of acknowledgement was significantly less deep and his eyes cooler than they had been when he was laughing with her a moment before.

"At your service, Miss Fernhill," he said, his voice managing to be chilly, reserved and ridiculously appealing all at the same time.

"Lord Hythe," she acknowledged, allowing her own voice to cool as she put her fingertips on his arm. If he owed her merely a modicum of courtesy, she could return the same. She was, after all, a viscount's daughter, even if one of questionable reputation.

Why was a man like the Earl of Hythe from a noble family who had apparently never had a stain on their cartouche at one of Lady Osborne's matchmaking house parties? Rilla would have to contain her curiosity. Even if he had not shown his disdain, that was not the kind of thing one asked a reserved gentleman.

He surprised her by making conversation. "Have you been to one of these house parties before?" The question could be borderline rude, since it implied that she had been trying and failing to find a husband. On the other hand, there was never any point in becoming annoyed about the truth.

"Never. In fact, this is only my second house party of any kind," she told him. "Which is why I was reluctant to leave my room."

This was a disaster. Had he known Miss Fernhill was going to be here, Hythe would never have come. They had never been introduced and she obviously did not recognise him, but he knew her.

At first, he had not realised, in the dim light of the passage, that it was her he found unexpectedly in his arms. She fitted. It was a ridiculous thing to say, and a worse thing to feel to the depths of his being. What did it mean? That she was the right height for him? That she was lithe and curvy, all at once? That something inside him recognised her, even before he knew who she was?

She had captured his attention from the beginning of the Season. Hythe had asked after her and discovered her scandalous mystery. No Belvoir countess could possibly have such question marks about her past. Hythe kept his distance, even though he had been drawn to her again and again when they happen to be at the same entertainments.

Now he was to be in her company for a week. Hythe should be calling for his carriage, and riding away from this place as fast as he could. Not promenading the lady through the house, as if she was any other gentlewoman.

Of course, he would treat her with every courtesy, even if having her so briefly in his arms had prompted thoughts that were far from polite. Apart from the necessary manners of a gentleman, he would simply have to avoid her, which would surely not be hard. Others would be at the house party, would they not?

It was with some relief that Hythe showed her into the drawing room, where a number of people had already gathered.

"Oh good," said the lady on his arm, "my cousin is already here." Hythe followed the direction of her gaze and saw the elderly matron who had been Miss Fernhill's chaperone throughout the

Season. Good indeed. His duty was almost done. He could safely conduct the lady to her cousin and hopefully stay far away from her for the remainder of the week.

It was only polite to linger long enough to acknowledge the introduction, then Lady Barker asked about his sister, Sophia, and so he remained to answer questions about the children. Lady Osbourne, their hostess, came and whisked Miss Fernhill away to introduce her to several of the other ladies, and Lady Barker saw somebody she knew and excused herself.

Now Hythe had exactly what he wanted; freedom to look about the room and contemplate the gathering. Why, then, was his gaze drawn inexorably to where Miss Fernhill was sitting on a sofa with another young lady, accepting introductions to various of the gentlemen?

But I saw her first, said some unruly ungovernable part of Hythe. Nonsense. He was a Belvoir. He was the Earl of Hythe. He would not forget what he owed to his name.

There was something appealing about the Earl of Hythe. Rilla had always thought so. Even when she was a shy little wall-flower making her debut in London for the first time. He had been far too young to be looking over the Season's crop of brides, but too serious minded and responsible to fit in easily with the boys of his own age.

This Season, she had seen him time and again, though they had never spoken. He had been unaware of her existence when she was a girl, and remained oblivious again this year.

Which was probably just as well, since her past made him as distant as a star floating high above lesser mortals. Rilla had no idea what he could possibly be doing at one of Lady Osborne's house parties. Surely, the Earl of Hythe needed no assistance to find a bride? Undoubtedly, he had to beat candidates off with a stick.

His motive was none of her business. She should be focusing on the other men. Men without a pristine family name. Men for whom her five thousand pounds outweighed where she might or might not have spent the last few years.

Once she had concluded she should avoid the man, Lady Osbourne confounded her by assigning Lord Hythe to escort Rilla in to dinner. Surely Lady Osborne did not expect a man like the very proper earl to make a match with someone with such a large question mark over her reputation? Whatever Lord Hythe thought about partnering her, he was gentleman enough to keep it to himself.

Indeed, she could not fault the man's manners. Very properly, he applied himself to conversation with her during the first course, starting with an innocuous hope that the weather, never certain in November, might nonetheless be kind to them for the next week.

"If not, my lord, Lady Osbourne has been telling the ladies we shall amuse ourselves indoors," she replied. Since he could not be a suitor, she allowed her true feelings to colour her next remark. "The delights she describes include charades, hide and seek, dancing, sharing our musical talents, treasure hunts, parlour games, and theatricals."

Lord Hythe bit back a groan.

She chuckled. "I am just as delighted at the prospect as you are, my lord."

His eyes twinkled at her, and she could not resist smiling back. "Dancing would not be so terrible," she acknowledged.

"Most of them would not be terrible if the others indulging in the activity have a modicum of talent," he replied. "For the sake of the audience, I shall do my best to avoid anything requiring me to sing or play a musical instrument."

Rilla nodded. "My Achilles heel is acting," she confided. She had reason to know that an audience of any size caused her to forget every line she had laboriously memorised. In addition, even in rehearsals, she had never been able to step inside a part.

"You need to let go of yourself and become someone else," Joseph had told her. Everyone around her seemed to find it easy, both in Society and in that other world. Rilla just went on being

Rilla. In the end, Joseph gave up on her and allowed her to contribute to their enterprise in other ways.

"Mind you," she told the earl, "I love a well-acted play. I so admire those who can draw us into a story so that we believe they really are Lady Macbeth tortured by guilt into madness, or Juliet, determined to die for love."

"It is especially impressive when the child-bride Juliet is played by a woman in her fourth or fifth decade, is it not?" Hythe replied. "To make us look past the mature form and see the slender innocent —there is a magic to it. I saw Emma Pilkington in the part this year. She is still a young woman, of course, just in her twenties, but she was clearly with child at the time. Within minutes, I had forgotten."

The Pilkingtons, husband and wife, had taken London by storm this year. Rilla had reason to know just how talented and creative they were.

"She has a gift," Rilla agreed. "The Pilkington company is built on her talent, and on her husband's strengths as a playwright and a producer."

Hythe nodded. "Society does not quite know what to make of them. An earl's daughter who made a runaway marriage and then went on the stage should not, in the public view, be a lady. But she and her husband are both well born and clearly devoted. Since they became reconciled with their families all but the high sticklers accept them."

"I do not suppose they care," Rilla observed. "They must be glad about their families, but for the rest? They have made their lives in the world of the theatre."

The servants were carrying away dishes and replacing them with those of the second remove. Hythe, with another charming smile, turned to address a remark to the lady on his other side. Rilla turned to her other dinner companion, who spent the next half hour telling her about his hounds and his hunting.

Lord Hythe might be totally off-limits as a suitor, but he was certainly an excellent dinner time conversationalist.

CHAPTER THREE

Certainly, the tale differs from house to house. So much so that Peggy Whitlow has not spoken to Maggie Cutler in three years since they came to hair-pulling and scratching when they were only fifteen over whether the white rider was an angel or the elf king. And many a promising pugilist has got his start in a dusty lane defending the honour of Miss Amaryllis from the accusation that she planned the whole thing.

["The Abduction of Amaryllis Fernhill", in *Collected Tales from the Villages of England*, by a Gentleman]

Hythe enjoyed the first remove at dinner far more than he had expected. Miss Fernhill was entertaining company with ideas of her own and not afraid to argue the point. Miss Fairleigh on his other side, whom Hythe quickly summed up as having more hair than wit, made the second half of the meal seem four times as long as the first. Their conversation was stilted until he threw out one of his prepared questions. "What do you like to do on a rainy day, Miss Fairleigh?"

After that, it took only the occasional comment to keep her prattling away about the relative merits of embroidery and water colours.

Hythe had two strong-minded sisters whom he respected and whose company enjoyed. He couldn't understand why Society saw any appeal in insipid young women who concurred with the opinion of any man who interested them. What could possibly make such females desirable as wives for any fellow with the least modicum of intelligence or any hope of the same for future children?

Why couldn't some of the eligible females be more like the very ineligible one he had brought in to dinner? On the other hand, perhaps Miss Fernhill had simplified Hythe's task. Perhaps he just needed to make it clear to the young ladies that, when he asked for an opinion, he was in earnest.

The following morning, when some of the party walked up a nearby prominence to admire the view, he tried the strategy on one of the young ladies. It was not a success. Hythe could not help but wonder whether her marriageability had been impaired by deep-rooted stupidity. The thought was not worthy of him.

Lunch had been set out on sideboards for people to serve themselves, with multiple tables around the room so people could sit in groups of up to ten. Hythe chose a seat at the same table as Miss Fernhill, desperate for some reasonable discourse. He could try again with some of the other lady guests, but for now it would be restful to spend time with someone who expected nothing from him.

Of course, several others joined the table and conversation remained trivial until someone made a disparaging remark about the ongoing debate on voting reform.

Miss Fernhill expressed an opinion. "We need to make sure that voters truly represent the population across the whole country," she said.

Miss Fairleigh asked, "Whatever do you mean, Miss Fernhill?"

"It is ridiculous that a large city like Manchester has no representatives in Parliament while a place like Dunwich returns two representatives. Dunwich has fewer than fifty people, and none of its thirty-two freemen voters actually live in Dunwich."

Hythe agreed. In medieval times, Dunwich been a thriving port with eight parishes, almost all now swallowed by the sea. The remaining half a parish nonetheless retained the right to send two members to Parliament, voted in by non-resident voters, half of them nominated by only two men.

Miss Fairleigh's fair brow furrowed. "I never worry about things like that."

Mr. Smythe chuckled. "No more you should, dear lady." He cast a censorious glance at Miss Fernhill. "We gentlemen do not expect ladies to be interested in politics."

Hythe maintained a calm visage despite a surge of rage. "I disagree," he said, and named at least three prominent politicians whose wives were at least as capable as their lords and were well-known in Society for the intelligent contributions they made to dinner parties and soirées.

To his surprise, his opinion made an immediate difference to the quality of the conversation, with several of the young ladies disclosing that they read the newspapers and thought about what was happening on the world scene.

Their table was soon full of vibrant discussion, and those without an interest in such things gravitated to the end furthest away with Hythe, no doubt to discuss the trivia that bored Hythe to tears.

Hythe enjoyed himself thoroughly, and felt very kindly towards Miss Fernhill for setting the scene. His positive view of her was enhanced when the pair of them fell into the sort of vigorous debate he enjoyed with his sisters and his closest friends. When he had to concede her point on one issue, he could not have been more pleased.

Rilla found lunch surprisingly delightful, thanks to Lord Hythe. Useful, too. Two of the men who had shown her some attention during the morning had drifted away when the discussion turned serious, one after expressing doubt that ladies were capable of intelligence.

The day continued fine enough to return outdoors, though clouds suggested that they would not be as fortunate the next day. Lady Osbourne suggested Rilla might like to take part in a game of pall mall. She had never played before, but the rules seemed straightforward enough.

One played in a pall mall alley, with walls on either side and an iron ring set in the ground around one hundred yards distant from where the players started. One used a mallet to hit a ball towards the ring, repeating the strokes until close. Then an implement with a spoon-like end was used to hit the ball through the ring.

It was harder than it looked to achieve the right direction and force. One of the other ladies playing, Miss Thompson, also claimed to be a novice, but Rilla soon guessed that the lady was pretending helplessness, presumably to impress the gentlemen.

Rilla came last in the first four contests, trailing one of the gentlemen, a Captain Hudson. "No room for a pall mall alley on a ship, Miss Fernhill," he said, cheerfully.

"I imagine that waves would also inhibit play, Captain Hudson," she replied, much to his amusement.

In the fifth contest, the others had once again finished before she and the captain were halfway down the alley. "I picked the game up quickly, did I not?" crowed Miss Thompson, whose combined scores made her third overall.

"I bet she is her village champion," muttered Captain Hudson. Rilla agreed, but pretended she hadn't heard.

Miss Thompson marched off on the arm of the overall winner, and the remaining couple came to let Rilla and Captain Hudson know they were going in out of the cold.

"Go ahead without us," Captain Hudson said. "Miss Fernhill and I have to find out who wins last place."

"It is a fight to the finish," Rilla agreed.

The other couple stayed to applaud each stroke, cheering when a wild stroke of Rilla's bounced off the alley walls and groaning when the captain's ball shot past the edge of the ring.

In the end, the captain finished first, but Rilla was only one stroke behind him. The other couple clapped, Rilla curtseyed, the captain bowed, and they all laughed.

A few spots of rain hurried their steps, and they left the alley behind in favour of a warm fire and a hot drink.

Captain Hudson, Rilla concluded, was a pleasant gentleman. He could laugh at himself, and he saw right through Miss Thompson. Rilla had no objection to a half-pay officer, though there was always the risk—presumably Captain Hudson would say the hope—he would be called back into service.

Did she want a husband in the armed forces, who was away more than he was at home?

This is only the first day of the house party, she reminded herself. She had plenty of time to consider that question. Which would not even be a question if he was simply being polite to the lady he had inadvertently been stuck with at the end of the pall mall alley.

However, when she came back downstairs after taking off her outer garments, he waved to catch her attention as she entered the drawing room. He had hot chocolate and cake waiting for her on a low table next to the chair he had been holding ready for her.

Surely that meant he was interested in pursuing the acquaintance?

He seems to be a nice man. He is a possibility. Then her eyes drifted to the man who had just come through the door. Lord Hythe. Her heart gave a bound. Stupid heart. Lord Hythe was not for the likes of her.

After lunch, Lord Hythe took one of the newspaper-reading maidens rowing on the lake, since the day was still fine enough for the exercise. Again, it was not a success, this time because of her opinions. She was happy to share with him her conviction that the lower classes needed a firm hand as they were predisposed to laziness and immorality, that showing leniency to thieves simply because they were children would lead to an increase in crime, and that extending the franchise would lead to anarchy and chaos.

It soon became clear that her views were a direct reflection of her father's and were not up for discussion. He wanted a wife who could think for herself, and he certainly didn't want an arch-Tory who was against everything he stood for.

He managed to remain civil, but was delighted when a few drops of rain heralded a shower, and he could pull back into the bank and escort her to the house. He remembered to thank her politely for her company. He would not be seeking it again.

He looked forward to dinner, hoping he would be partnered again with Miss Fernhill, but instead Lady Osbourne had changed all of the assignments. He suffered through another hour and a half of inane conversation about the weather, fashion, and the latest London gossip, and was relieved to be left at the table to have port with the gentlemen.

He would not join the ladies again tonight, he decided. He finished his port and made his farewells. He was halfway up the stairs to his room when he realised he had left his gloves behind. As he opened the door to the dining room, Miss Fernhill's name caught his attention and he paused to listen. Eavesdropping was reprehensible, but too tempting to resist.

Three of the other gentlemen were talking about her in admiring tones—her grace, her beauty, her intelligence. When the man who had partnered her for dinner tentatively suggested that she was less than reputable, one of her admirers insisted that, if she was good enough for a high stickler for Lord Hythe, she certainly merited the consideration of less elevated gentlemen.

Good. If he had done the lady a favou r, he was glad of it. He had no feelings at all about her being courted by another man. Of course, he didn't.

CHAPTER FOUR

Still, everyone in the village knows the essence of the tale, whether they were in the church on that day years ago or not. The bride, plain, pale-faced and drooping. The groom with his face set like stone. The bride's uncle chivvying them up the aisle. Then the west transept doors crashing open (some say exploding, but if so, the villagers did a good job of repair, for there they are today for any child to see, ancient oak, worn by time).

["The Abduction of Amaryllis Fernhill", in Collected Tales from the Villages of England, by a Gentleman]

The following day was stormy—far too cold, wet, and windy for any further ventures outside.

As Rilla had predicted, Lady Osbourne was keen to marshal her guests into group activities. Thankfully, she left the guests themselves to choose between the pursuits on offer, though any lady or gentleman without an occupation was politely rounded up and channelled into being sociable.

Rilla avoided the room where an excited group were planning a theatrical performance, and also backed quickly from the one that contained a game of charades.

She would have liked to play billiards. She'd learned the game from her best friend, the daughter of the earl whose estate bordered her father's, and had continued to play on her own after Emma made a runaway marriage. But not after her father died and her uncle moved into her house. He did not approve of females playing billiard. Doubtless, the gentlemen at this house party would agree.

Was Lord Hythe in the billiards room? She had not seen him playing cards and could not imagine him as part of the laughing, flirting parlour games crowd. Perhaps, although he had denied any musical abilities, he formed part of the audience in the music room? She found herself heading in that direction and stopped.

What was she doing? She needed to be somewhere Lord Hythe was not. When he was in the vicinity, she found it impossible to consider any other man. And Lord Hythe was not for her.

She had to move to the side of the passage to make way for several of the guests, ladies and gentlemen, who were hurrying to find hiding places for a game of sardines. Another activity that was not to Rilla's taste. At the previous house party she had attended, she had found herself stuck in a cupboard under the stairs with four other people, one of whom had wandering hands.

In the end, Rilla collected her embroidery from her room, and joined Cousin Felicia in the parlour. Several gentlemen had also joined the ladies. Captain Hudson was whittling, and was happy to explain he was making a set of wooden soldiers for his older brother's eldest son. "I suggested sailors," he joked, "but apparently it has to be soldiers." Rilla joined the others in admiring the skill with which he crafted a detailed little warrior out of a chunk of wood. "They will look more realistic once they are painted," he told his audience.

Another gentleman was sketching the ladies as they worked. He asked Rilla if he could make a sketch of her hands, as they were particularly elegant. Rilla would have brushed it off as a meaningless compliment, but Mr. Woolard's gaze at said appendages had a dispassionate quality that hinted his interest was entirely artistic. She granted permission.

Lord Joseph Enright said he had no skills to craft anything with his hands, but offered to read to the company. Lord Joseph was the second son of a marquis, but seemed to have avoided the arrogance that often went with such elevated rank. He had a very pleasant voice, and read with a dramatic style that suited the Robert Burns poem he had chosen, Tam O'Shanter.

Rilla did not understand some of the Scottish words, but she laughed with the others at the tale of the drunken Scotsman spying on a witches' gathering, becoming entranced at the dancing of 'a winsome wench' and calling out encouragement. Then followed a wild chase until at last his brave horse managed to cross water, just in time to escape the lead witch, though the poor nag paid for its master's peeping by the loss of its tail.

"What is a cutty sark," she asked, when everyone had clapped the ending of the piece. "Does anyone know?"

Miss MacRae, one of the chaperones, was able to explain. "A sark is a shirt; in this case, a night-rail. Cutty simply means short, Miss Fernhill."

"She was dancing in her night attire, then, and it flapped as she danced," Captain Hudson chuckled. "No wonder naughty Tam was glued to the peephole in the wall."

Rilla suppressed her smile when several of the ladies called him to account, and poor Lord Joseph, as well, for reading the poem in mixed company. Rilla was pleased to note that neither gentleman seemed much abashed. Certainly, she had heard far more bawdy stories in the world that had been her refuge from her uncle's machinations.

Hythe made the excuse of correspondence and sequestered himself in his room until the afternoon. *You will not find a wife in your bed chamber, he told himself.* Then, remembering some of the stories he had heard about house parties, *not one you want, that is.*

He locked his door and went down to join the rest of the company for afternoon tea, determined to spend time with the young ladies he had not yet met.

The prettiest of the bunch was Miss Fairleigh. In Hythe's opinion, her good looks and pleasant nature did not outweigh her inability to hold a reasonable conversation. Second runner-up was a damsel by the name of Miss Turnbull. She had the much-admired English rose complexion and colouring, and her fashionably-gowned figure was shapely and graceful. Hythe inserted himself into the crowd of men around her.

Poor lady. The other men in the group were a bunch of pompous boors. The talk was all about fashion and the fashionable set. Twaddle. Hythe contained himself. It remained to be seen whether Miss Turnbull actually enjoyed such trivial conversation, or whether she was merely displaying excellent breeding and deportment. He would have to talk to her away from her other admirers.

Meanwhile, Miss Fernhill had her own covey of gentlemen. Or, to be exact, she and a couple of other ladies, including Miss Fairleigh. Hythe couldn't help but notice that they were enjoying themselves a lot more than he was. He could not in all honesty claim that Miss Fernhill was as pretty as Miss Fairleigh and Miss Turnbull. So why could he not get her out of his mind?

CHAPTER FIVE

The storytellers agree on the troop of riders. Did they trot or gallop or merely walk in through the great doors?

They were beautiful, all make that clear, and the man (or angel or devil or elf-king) at their head was the loveliest of all. Dressed in white, crowned in gold, with long flowing locks. Jewels glittered from rings and brooches and even the cuffs of his boots. A long cloak (or perhaps wings) streamed behind him.

["The Abduction of Amaryllis Fernhill", in *Collected Tales from the Villages of England*, by a Gentleman]

The example of Lord Hythe, Lord Joseph, and Captain Hudson had apparently turned the tide in Rilla's favour. But as such things go, something gained was balanced by something lost. The more respectful and attentive the men grew, the more defensive and difficult became the ladies.

Several days into the party, Rilla had grown tired of conversations that stopped as soon as she got near, and of ignoring pointed remarks about jilts muttered just loud enough for her to hear.

Miss Thompson, in particular, sharpened her words with darts aimed precisely at Rilla's vulnerabilities. Little remarks, delivered in a sweet tone, always with a wide blue-eyed innocence.

"One must trust one's elders to know what is best for one. Do you not agree? If one's guardian—one's uncle, for example, makes a match, it behoves a lady to be grateful." "A lady's reputation is her most important asset, and anything is preferable to the loss of it." "A large dowry will cover a multitude of sins, I suppose."

The sly looks at Rilla confirmed that she was the targets of these nuggets of wisdom. Rilla ignored both remarks and looks. Miss Thompson's nastiness brought its own punishment. Rilla had watched her sabotage her chances with one gentleman after another, as she exercised her malicious wit in their presence. Mr. Smythe was the only admirer she had left, and the pair of them deserved one another.

However, Rilla felt impelled to intercede when Miss Thompson turned her tongue on Miss Fairleigh. Miss Fairleigh might not be the brightest button in the box, but she was friendly and eager to please. Miss Thompson apparently found these traits objectionable.

Rilla ignored the remarks that Miss Fairleigh was too innocent or not clever enough to notice. Indeed, they became a useful barometer. Those who laughed were not worth Rilla's time, and the gentlemen who looked most disgusted or uncomfortable were those Rilla favoured with her own attention.

However, one afternoon, Miss Fairleigh was packing the tea things neatly on to a tray. Miss Thompson said, "In the name of the Good Lord, Miss Fairleigh, are you trying to do the servants out of a job?"

Miss Fairleigh bit at her lower lip, a sure sign that she was perturbed. "Why no, Miss Thompson. The servants are very busy, however, with all the guests. I thought to be kind." She turned to Rilla. "Might a servant be dismissed if I help, Miss Fernhill?"

Rilla reassured her. "No, indeed, Miss Fairleigh. I am sure they appreciate your kindness in tidying up after our tea. May I pass you some cups?"

Miss Fairleigh smiled beatifically. "Mama says that the path to Heaven is paved with little acts of kindness," she confided.

Miss Thompson's gaze sharpened. "Kindness won't save you if you associate with the wrong sort of people, Miss Fairleigh," she warned, turning to glare at Rilla in case anyone in the audience did not understand what she meant.

"I daresay you would consider the Lord Jesus the wrong sort of people, Miss Thompson, since Miss Fairleigh is tidying the tea cups for him."

Miss Thompson wiped her momentary confusion away with smug contempt. "I have no idea what that person is talking about." She never addressed Rilla directly. "Except I am sure my governess warned me about taking the Lord's name in vain," she added, and she composed her expression into one of pious superiority.

Lord Joseph Enright chuckled. "Rather brilliant of you, Miss Fernhill. *When you do this for the least of my children, you do it for me.* Right?"

He sent his smile around the rest of group. "Miss Fernhill is pointing out the passage in the Gospels where Jesus indicates that lack of charity is the worst sin of all, and I must agree, Miss Fairleigh. Your kindness is an example to us all.

Lord Joseph's father the marquis had recently been raised from a vicarage to the peerage on the death of his cousin. The young ladies therefore swallowed his opinion with every appearance of compliance, and afterwards were markedly kinder to Miss Fairleigh.

F our days into the interminable week, Hythe had made no progress in his bride hunt. It had taken him the space of an afternoon to discover that Miss Thompson was an unkind shrew, and if he doubted his own experience, the men who knew her from London confirmed it. One by one, he spent a little time with each lady at the house party. This girl was too frivolous. That one was waspish.

In any case, he did not find himself in the least attracted to any of them. Surely it was not too much to ask that the woman to whom he would vow to be faithful for the remainder of their days was one he actually wanted to bed? He could not imagine physical intimacies with any of the ladies currently on offer.

Except Miss Fernhill. She had grown prettier day by day—not the flashy kind of beauty some of the others had, but a quiet loveliness that comprised her character as well as her features. Her attractions were manifold, and not least of them was her mind. She commanded his attention whenever she was in the vicinity. Even when she wasn't, he could not stop thinking about her.

Perhaps he was making things worse by spending so much time with her. But nobody else here challenged him to think the way she did. When he succeeded in winning a discussion point with her, he felt as if he had persuaded the entire House of Lords— yes, and the Austrian and Prussian negotiators.

What an ambassador for Britain, she would have been, if she'd been a man. She knew several languages, understood the current political situation better most people of his acquaintance, male or female, and was invariably charming and composed.

The company that had been inclined at first to treat her with disdain was now, with few exceptions, thoroughly enjoying her company, and at least two of the gentlemen were seriously considering a courtship. Hythe felt she could do better than a penniless second son or a half-pay naval captain, but at least the lady would have choices.

Last night, those two gentlemen had discussed their inclination with the assembly, and Hythe had learned a little more about the circumstances surrounding Miss Fernhill's disappearance.

Mr. Smythe had challenged Captain Hudson's interest in the lady. "Surely, you would not wish to marry someone who jilted her betrothed at the altar?" he jeered. "Would you not fear the same treatment?"

"If she accepted my suit, she would have no reason to jilt me," the captain replied. "I am not nearly in my dotage, riddled with the pox, and suspected of beating a previous wife to death, and I have no intention of forcing her to the altar by threats against her virtue."

"You are right about Baron Hargreaves, her betrothed," said one of the other men. "I wouldn't let him within a mile of a sister of mine, if I had one."

She had been betrothed to Baron Hargreaves? Hythe knew the man and his ghastly son. He wished he didn't. They were a scourge on the aristocracy—the sort of slimy worm who thought being noble and male entitled them to take whatever and whomever they wanted, whether welcome or not.

"How do you know she was being forced?" Lord Joseph asked.

The informed man shrugged. "The baron's son drinks to excess. Has always done so, but even more since his… er… accident."

Most of the gentlemen sniggered, though they all winced, too. The marquis's son asked for an explanation, which the man provided. "Hargreaves Fili assaulted the wrong woman. She reinforced her refusal with a poker, with enough force to render her assailant unable to ever again enjoy his favourite activity."

Lord Joseph worked that out and joined the wincing. Hythe thought Alfred Hargreaves got just what he deserved.

Hythe had known the story of the supposed abduction from the church, but not the name of the prospective groom and the pressure applied to Miss Fernhill. He had no idea how she had found a way out of her dilemma, but he admired her more than ever.

Unfortunately, his admiration wasn't enough. Most of Society was happy to blame her entirely for not accepting the marriage thrust upon her. Hythe must not forget he was responsible for keeping up the family name.

His political clout depended on the quality and probity of the countess he chose. His future children depended on their mother's reputation.

On the other hand, his sister Sophia had married James— against Hythe's advice— when there was still some question about his legitimacy. After he had been recognised as the firstborn and legitimate son of the Duke of Winshire, more cautious maidens complained she had stolen a march on them. She had not done it as a strategy, but because she was in love.

James was just as besotted with Sophia. Hythe had been wrong.

As for his sister Felicity, her marriage would be scandalous yet had she not been a Belvoir, and had he and Sophia not accepted her rascal of a husband as their new brother. Felicity was also driven by love, and Hythe had to admit that Justin loved Felicity just as deeply.

Three years of Miss Fernhill's life were missing. Could that be ignored? Could the combined weight of his friends and family make her an acceptable bride for the Earl of Hythe?

I don't care. The thought came out of nowhere and was shocking in its certainty. Hythe rolled it around in his mind and said it out loud. "I don't care?" The answer was instant. *I don't care. What matters is not what anyone else thinks or says. She is my match in every way that matters.*

His cautious side whispered *Three. Years.* True. He did need to know Miss Fernhill well enough to ask her about those three years. Deep down, he was sure she had done nothing disreputable, and he would certainly defend her to anyone who asked. But he would like to know.

CHAPTER SIX

The old folks are in unison again on the bride's reaction. "She came alive," says Granny Smithers. "Straightened. Smiled with such joy that she looked beautiful for the first time in her life, poor lady."

["The Abduction of Amaryllis Fernhill", in *Collected Tales from the Villages of England,* by a Gentleman]

The focus of the house party had changed. For the first three days, Lady Osbourne had organised them into activities, making certain that each lady was partnered with a gentleman, and that the pairings changed frequently in the course of each day.

On the fourth day, she made it clear that, if any gentlemen had a particular interest in a lady, he should speak with her privately, and she would ensure that the pair were given time together. She likewise asked the ladies to privately tell her if there was any gentleman they wished to avoid.

The Earl of Hythe was the only person Rilla was drawn to. She was not going to make a fool of herself by telling Lady Osbourne. Perhaps Lord Joseph or Captain Hudson would ask for more time with her, and if so, she would give them serious consideration. She wasn't a child to refuse a pleasant marriage because she could not have the dream of love.

If she did not find a husband at this party, she needed to seek employment. She was almost through the money she had saved, and she had no intention of living off Cousin Felicia, whose mere competence would not spread to the two of them. She must forget about Lord Hythe and focus her attentions on those who might seek to take her to wife.

And if no one suitable asked her, it did not mean her dreams of marriage and motherhood were dead. Housekeepers sometimes married. Rarely, it was true, but it did happen.

However, that afternoon when the showers cleared, Lord Hythe asked her if she would join a group who were walking to the top of the nearby hill, which gave a view out over the estate. Furthermore, when the party split into couples, each gentleman escorting a lady, Rilla found herself on Lord Hythe's arm.

"It is good to get out in the fresh air," she said to him.

"Yes," he agreed. "Especially in the country."

"Do you prefer the country, Lord Hythe?" How sad, if so, for by all accounts, he spent most of his time in cities.

He confirmed rumour by saying, "I love to be in the country, but most Parliamentary work is done in London, and when that work sends me overseas, it is usually to cities."

She voiced her thought. "How sad."

Lord Hythe shrugged. "It was a choice," he said. "I love my work, Miss Fernhill. I am good at it and it makes a difference."

They reached a flight of steps that would take them up a steep slope onto the hill path. Most of the rest of the party were well ahead, for Lord Hythe had set a slow pace. Even the footman had passed them.

"That is good, then." Rilla said, wondering if he had deliberately delayed them.

"My country estate is my retreat," he confided. "I spend a few weeks there several times a year, though last time was not the same."

A note in his voice had her searching his expression, but it gave away nothing of his thoughts. Was it sorrow? Impatience? Irritation, perhaps?

"What about you, Miss Fernhill?" he asked. "Do you prefer the country?"

"I have little with which to compare it, my lord," Rilla confided. She might as well be honest with the man. "My first Season in London when I was seventeen was not a success, which undoubtedly coloured my thinking. Apart from that and a few months this year, I have lived all my life in the country."

"Lady Barker lives near York," he commented.

"Near, not in," she said. "She and I did make several trips to York when I was preparing for my Season, but I cannot say I know the town well."

Lord Hythe was not going to let the topic go, clearly. "Did you find London as disappointing this time?"

Rilla's first instinct was to say she did. Her ruined reputation had come before her and made ton events an ordeal rather than a pleasure. But there was also much about London that she liked. "I found the theatre, the museums, and many other things about London very enjoyable."

A couple of drops of rain fell, but before they could react, the footman coming running back down the path to give them an umbrella. "Back to the house or on up the hill," Lord Hythe asked, once he had put it up.

The footman was hurrying back up the hill, presumably to make sure that everyone else was dry, but the rain was barely a drizzle, and certainly not sufficient to drive Rilla back inside.

"Onward and upward," she proclaimed.

Lord Hythe smiled. "Good choice."

"What made your latest stay in the country less satisfactory, my lord?" Rilla asked. She watched a frown crease his brow. "If it is not an impertinent question."

"Not impertinent," he assured her, his frown clearing. "Indeed, it is very pertinent. Mine is not a large family, Miss Fernhill, but I have two sisters whom I love dearly. My younger sister has been my chatelaine and my hostess since my older sister married. Now that Felicity has wed, I felt lonely in the country."

"And so, you decided to find a wife," she said, her mouth running ahead of her wits. "I do apologise, Lord Hythe. I should not have spoken that thought out loud."

He chuckled. "Your conclusion is correct, or at least partly correct. I need a wife for many reasons, not least for companionship. I decided that the time had come."

They reached the lookout, and their tête-à-tête had to give way to a more general group conversation, but Lord Hythe's willingness to talk about his sisters and his wife hunt had given Rilla much to think about. Could Lord Hythe possibly be courting her?

Hythe thought Miss Fernhill might return to the question of his search for a wife as they continued their walk over the crest of the hill and down the other side. Tucked under the umbrella together, they could not have been more private.

Instead, they talked about the slave trade. Miss Fernhill thought it was not enough to stop the sale of human beings, but that slavery itself should be outlawed in all British territories. Hythe agreed with her, but they disagreed about how that happy state could be achieved.

"Politics is the art of the possible, Miss Fernhill," he told her.

"Unless we start with the ideal, Lord Hythe," she retorted, "how will we ever discover what is possible?"

Back at the house, they separated to change and then met again to play chess in the library, one of several couples quietly pursuing a better acquaintance over a game board or a pack of cards. Miss Fernhill proved to be a worthy opponent., checkmating him after an intensive tussle.

After that, Hythe had to surrender her to Captain Hudson, who must have persuaded Lady Osbourne to give him a chance with the lady. Hythe made sure to remedy his oversight by asking his hostess to partner him with Miss Fernhill for dinner for the remainder of the week.

Either Lady Osbourne had already made up her mind to help him or she took pity on him, for he found himself next to Miss Fernhill when he took his seat. For the first remove, good manners required him to pay attention to the young lady he had escorted to the table.

Then came the second remove. "Miss Fernhill," he said, turning to her. "May I interest you in another walk tomorrow morning? I believe the circuit around the lake is very nice. And perhaps chess again in the afternoon?"

Captain Hudson looked back over his shoulder to narrow his eyes at Hythe before returning his attention to the lady on the other side of him. Good. Let the good captain be on notice that he had competition for Miss Fernhill's hand.

Serious competition, for Hythe did not discount the lure of his title. On the other hand, he had a feeling Miss Fernhill did not care about titles. Still, she had agreed to both of his suggestions about tomorrow, so she must have at least a modicum of interest, even if Hythe lacked the address of a certain bedamned dashing naval officer.

CHAPTER SEVEN

The rider, without stopping, stretched out his hand and Miss Amaryllis reached up and took it, put her foot on his in the stirrup, and was riding into the east transept before the elderly groom had picked up his dropped jaw.

["The Abduction of Amaryllis Fernhill", in *Collected Tales from the Villages of England*, by a Gentleman]

If the Earl of Hythe was not courting Rilla, he was making it quite impossible for anyone else to do so. He had sought her out two days in row, paying her such marked attention that Lord Joseph and Captain Hudson had both turned their sights to other ladies.

Some of the ladies had not taken his marked interest in Rilla as gracefully as those two gentlemen. Miss Turnbull, in particular, made every effort to take Rilla's place. "Lord Hythe! I have saved you a seat." "Lord Hythe, will you turn the pages for me as I play?" "Lord Hythe, I feel a little faint. Will you not offer me your arm?"

Lord Hythe proved himself to be a diplomat and a politician, turning each request politely aside by declaring that he was currently escorting Miss Fernhill, and offering one of the other gentlemen as a substitute. By the second day of his determined avoidance of the lady, her seething rage was barely contained, and her nasty remarks had become louder and more pointed.

Rilla did her best to avoid her, even to the extent of whisking herself behind the curtains of a bow window when she heard Miss Turnbull's voice coming towards her along the otherwise deserted passage in the ladies' bedroom wing.

"He would have to marry me then, Mother, wouldn't he," said Miss Turnbull, gleefully.

Mrs. Turnbull's reply was little more than a mumble.

"I shall be very careful," Miss Turnbull assured her. "I shall pick a moment when no one is in the gentlemen's wing."

Mrs. Turnbull said something, but the only clear words were: "risk" and "ruined".

"He is a gentleman, Mother," Miss Turnbull said, carelessly. "He is known for doing the correct thing. And it is worth the risk. He is the most eligible man at the house…"

Her voice trailed off as a door opened then closed. Rilla slipped out from behind the curtain and went downstairs. The man they spoke of must be Lord Hythe, who was clearly the most eligible man at the house party. Rilla would have to warn him! He was currently out riding in the rain with some of the other gentlemen, but surely there would be an opportunity this afternoon to have a private word?

With the Turnbull vixen in hot pursuit, Hythe had taken to making sure he had a witness wherever he went. Miss Fernhill, for preference. Otherwise, one of the other gentlemen, even when, as now, he was returning to his bedchamber to change out of the wet clothes he had worn riding that morning.

An overreaction, perhaps, since Pritchard would be waiting for him. However, Hythe would confirm the valet's presence—and the absence of anyone else—before he allowed the amiable Lord Joseph to wander on his way.

"Give me a moment more of your time, Lord Joseph," he said, as he unlocked the door, "and I shall fetch that volume of poetry I mentioned."

He swung the door wide and stepped aside to let Lord Joseph go first, then had to pull up short when Lord Joseph stopped in his tracks. "Good Lord!"

Hythe recognised the shrill voice from the direction of his bed. "Lord Joseph. But isn't this Lord Hythe's bedroom?" Hythe looked around the marquis's son. Miss Turnbull was just pulling his sheets up to cover her naked breasts.

Miss Turnbull's eyes lit up and her shriek changed to a purr, accompanied by a coy look beneath her lashes. "Hythe, darling. Here you are at last."

"Forget it, Miss Turnbull," Hythe told her. "You have not compromised me, which is what you no doubt intended. Come, Lord Joseph, we will wait in the hall while Miss Turnbull dresses and leaves."

Before the two men could step out of the room, another shriek sounded behind them. "My poor little girl! Lord Hythe, you monster, what have you done?"

This is all it needs. Mrs. Turnbull, accompanied by Lady Osbourne, filled the doorway.

Mrs. Turnbull's eyes fell on the marquis's son. "Lord Joseph, what are you doing here?" *And the drama becomes a farce.*

Lord Joseph examined his fingernails. "Apparently, I am bearing witness that Lord Hythe has not compromised your daughter. You must be delighted, Mrs. Turnbull, to know your daughter is still in the same state of innocence that was hers when she somehow managed to enter the locked bedroom of a gentleman who has been out riding all morning."

Lord Joseph had been an inspired choice as company. Hythe's usual hard-won address had abandoned him in his anger at the invasion of his privacy and the attempt to bully him into matrimony. 'In the same state of innocence', indeed!

"Maude," Lady Osbourne said, "help your daughter get dressed, and take her to my private sitting room. Gentlemen, we shall leave them to it, if you please."

Mrs. Turnbull was not quite ready to give up. "Lord Hythe must have invited her here," she insisted. "He has ravaged my poor daughter." She howled the last few words and dabbed her handkerchief to a dry eye.

Lady Osbourne was not sympathetic. "Do not be more ridiculous than you can help, Maude. As things are, I am sure Lord Hythe and Lord Joseph can be persuaded to keep this incident quiet. Make a fuss, and the girl shall be ruined. Do you want to be shunned from London Society, you and your whole family?"

Hythe decided it was time to speak up. "I did not make an assignation with your daughter. I have taken pains not to be alone with of the young ladies at this house party. I will not marry Miss Turnbull under any circumstances. I *will* keep this incident between ourselves, provided that the pair of you remove yourselves and say nothing further."

Lord Joseph shrugged. "I won't tell anybody," he said.

Mrs. Turnbull's shoulders slumped, and she turned back towards her daughter. As the other three exited into the passage, and Hythe closed the door, he heard Miss Turnbull say, "But Mother, you said..."

"Foolish pair," said Lady Osbourne. "I apologise, Lord Hythe. Lord Joseph, I am glad you were present when Lord Hythe returned to his room. You may be sure I will interrogate the servants to discover who gave that foolish young lady the key to your room."

At that moment, Pritchard scurried along the passage with Hythe's washing water, slowing as he realised that his master and two other gentlefolk stood in the passage outside Hythe's room. "My lady. My lords."

"A small pest infestation," Hythe told Pritchard. "It is being removed. Pass me the jug, Pritchard, if you would. I will wait here while you fetch me a cup of tea to have while I dress." Best if the only witnesses to Miss Turnbull's exit were those who already knew about the escapade.

The valet bowed, but set the jug on a nearby hall table. "I will carry it inside when I return, my lord." He hurried away.

The door opened, and Mrs. Turnbull peeped out and then stepped into the passage, followed by her daughter. They did not look at Hythe or Lord Joseph. Mrs. Turnbull glared at Lady Osbourne and opened her mouth, then thought better of whatever she was going to say and led her daughter away.

Lord Joseph inclined his head. "The Keats, Hythe?"

"Of course," Hythe agreed, picking up the jug of hot water and leading the way into his room.

When Lord Hythe came down to lunch, he clearly had something on his mind, but whatever it was, he shook it off and was his usual charming company. When Lady Osbourne stood to invite them all to choose their afternoon activity, Hythe was ready with a suggestion.

"Miss Fernhill, may I escort you for a walk in the picture gallery?"

Rilla swallowed her instant agreement to give the approved response. "I will need to ask my cousin."

Cousin Felicia insisted on coming with them, but then declared she was too tired for the long promenade, and would seat herself at one end of the gallery where she could watch the couple from a distance.

They set off down the gallery, Rilla on Hythe's arm. Wall sconces lit the paintings, and what daylight there was filtered in through the windows, so they moved from pool of light to shadows and then back into a pool of light.

Rilla waited for Hythe to raise whatever topic was on his mind.

Surely, he was not about to propose? If he did, what would she say? She knew he was an honourable man and a kind one. Was that enough?

The problem was, she liked Hythe too much to saddle him with a wife like her. She would have to refuse him, and then she would have to explain to Cousin Felicia why she had refused him.

For several minutes, Hythe made comments about the various paintings in the gallery. Rilla responded in kind. How foolish she was to think a man like Hythe was interested in a woman like her. He had clearly just latched onto her to defend himself from the crazy antics of those desperate enough to try to trap him into marriage.

It was unfortunate for Rilla, since her other suitors had melted away at his supposed competition, but she could not blame him.

Which reminded her of what she overheard that morning. "Lord Hythe, I heard part of a conversation when I went up to get my shawl before lunch. I think it was about you. Just in case, may I suggest that you take someone with you when you return to your bedchamber tonight, and that you lock the door and perhaps put something against it?"

Hythe stopped in his tracks and looked down at her. He had his polite blank face on.

Rilla hastened to add, "They might not have been talking about you, of course. They just said the most eligible man at the house party."

"Someone else is planning a compromise?" Hythe asked. "Who was it?"

Rilla hesitated. "I would rather not name names; in case I am wrong. Wait a minute. You said someone else?"

Hythe nodded. "When I went up to dress after riding, I found someone waiting in my room. Fortunately, I had been out all morning, and had Lord Joseph with me when I opened the door. Her mo– her chaperone turned up a moment or two later, with Lady Osbourne."

"But that is what I heard them plotting," Rilla said. "I am so glad you had Lord Joseph with you, my lord."

His smile looked smug to Rilla. "Are you? Is there a particular reason?"

"Should there be?" she asked. "I would not wish anyone to be forced into marriage with someone unsuitable."

The smug look vanished. "Baron Hargreaves," he said. "I heard. For what it is worth, I think you did the right thing. Not that I know what you did. But Baron Hargreaves? What was your uncle thinking?"

"He was thinking that the baron would pay him the value of my dowry." Rilla growled. "The baron only wanted a brood mare, and he had run out of other options. No one would marry him from choice, and nor would any parent who cared about their daughter agree to such a match."

Hythe nodded. "Especially after the death of his third wife," he agreed. "You should get a medal."

That was a surprise. No one had ever suggested that Rilla was justified in running away from her unwanted marriage. Even Cousin Felicia, who said she understood, still accepted that Rilla was ruined as a result.

"Thank you," Rilla said. "And thank you, too, Lord Hythe, for being so nice to me during this last week. I've enjoyed our times together."

"Have you?" he asked. "Enough to come to Belvoir Close for two weeks in December?"

"Come to…?" Rilla stopped walking to look down the long gallery to where Cousin Felicia was chatting with the footman. She looked back up at Hythe. Was she awake? Or was this a dream?

"I should like you to meet my sisters and their families, and to show you my family home," he said.

Rilla frowned. "Lord Hythe, are you courting me?"

He grimaced. "Obviously not very well, if you have to ask. What did you think I was doing?"

She replied instantly. "Spending time with a friend while avoiding marriage-minded females and their chaperones."

He nodded. "That, too, but it would have been the act of a cad to pay you special attention if I did not wish to explore whether we might have a future together. You had no idea?"

"What of my reputation, Lord Hythe?" she asked.

Hythe bowed his head to look at his boots. "I think I have come to know you a little over the past week, Miss Fernhill." He met her gaze, his own intent. "I find it hard to believe you have done anything that would give me cause to change my mind about seeking your hand."

Rilla was touched, but thought he might be overstating the case. Would he really want to marry her when he knew the truth? There was only one way to find out.

Hythe spoke before she could. "Will you come to Belvoir Close?" he asked.

Rilla made up her mind. "I believe I must tell you the whole of my story before I do, Lord Hythe. You can then withdraw your invitation, if you so wish, without inconveniencing yourself or embarrassing your sisters."

At that moment, half a dozen of the other guests entered the gallery, and began walking towards Rilla and Lord Hythe.

"We shall find a way to talk in private," Hythe promised. "I must admit it will ease my mind to know what we have to work with when it comes to guiding public opinion."

"Guiding public opinion?" she asked, the word "we" warming her heart.

But the others were upon them, and their private conversation was over.

CHAPTER EIGHT

Some say the bridegroom stood there, frozen. Some that he tried to drag her down from the horse and was shouldered aside by the following riders. However it might have been, the eastern doors opened as mysteriously as the west, and closed behind the riders with a loud bang, and open they would not, not for all the trying in the world.

["The Abduction of Amaryllis Fernhill", in *Collected Tales from the Villages of England*, by a Gentleman]

Miss Turnbull and her mother were conspicuous by their absence throughout the afternoon. After her conversation with Hythe, Rilla wondered if they had left the house party early, but Lady Osbourne gave no explanation.

It was the last afternoon, and something of a frantic mood had descended on the house party, as if the guests sought to pour another week's worth of activities into the remaining hours. Lord

Hythe invited Rilla to play chess. The library was full of other people, and they had no chance for private conversation.

She suggested a stroll in the conservatory, thinking the chill might keep others away, but three other couples clearly had the same idea.

Lord Hythe noted that the sun had come out and asked her for a walk on the terrace. Mr. Smythe overheard and announced it to the room, and half the ladies in the place hurried upstairs to collect their coats, shawls and bonnets.

The fresh air was welcome, if a bit crisp. They did not stay out for long, returning to the drawing room where Lord Joseph read to the assembly again, this time from the poet Keats, and Miss Fairleigh sang a moving ballad about unrequited love.

When Rilla and Cousin Felicia returned to their bedchamber to prepare for dinner, the maid they shared was standing in the centre of the room, her mouth agape. Around her was chaos—the clothes from their trunks and the dressing area scattered across the floor, pages torn from the book Rilla had borrowed from the library screwed up and thrown down on top of the clothes, an indescribable stench arising from where chamber pots had been tipped upside down on the beds.

Cousin Felicia sent her to fetch Lady Osbourne. "Touch nothing, Amaryllis. We shall step into the hall and wait for our hostess.

Lady Osbourne was suitably horrified. "I have never had anything like this happen at one of my house parties before," she assured Cousin Felicia. "I will move you to another room, of course, and my servants will go to work straight away cleaning and pressing your garments. Meanwhile, I am sure we can find something for you both to wear down to dinner."

Cousin Felicia was furious. Rilla thought she should be, too, but mostly the malice in the attack made her feel sick. Whoever it was— and she had little doubt it was Miss Thompson—had torn or broken what she could, and poured ink and the contents of several chamber pots over what remained.

Their jewellery was intact, but Cousin Felicia's skin preparations and Rilla's perfume had been spilled into the mess.

"I am sorry about your book, Lady Osbourne," she said to her hostess.

"You have nothing to apologise for," Lady Osbourne insisted. "It is the fault of the person who is responsible for this outrage. I believe it to have been another of the guests, who left the house at my request earlier this afternoon. Undoubtedly, she could not have accomplished this without making several trips. One of the servants will be able to confirm her identity, and then I shall know what to do next. She will, I assure you, be sorry."

It was Miss Turnbull, then. Rilla shuddered. The woman must be unbalanced. Lord Hythe had had a lucky escape.

Miss Fernhill appeared pale when she came down to dinner, and Lady Barker had a grim look about her that worried Hythe. He had no chance to ask Miss Fernhill what was going on, though. She and Lady Barker had appeared just as dinner was announced, and Lady Osbourne had already asked him to escort Miss Fairleigh.

He applied himself to conversation with the pretty blonde, though he could not resist a few glances at Miss Fernhill. She was sitting between Lord Joseph and Captain Hudson, which worried Hythe. Was Lady Barker opposed to his suit? Was Lady Osbourne?

He would take his dismissal if he must, but only from Miss Fernhill herself. She was, after all, of age. She was also looking more cheerful, and not once that he saw did she look his way.

"You like her, do you not?" said Miss Fairleigh.

Hythe flushed. It was the height of poor manners to ignore his dinner partner to stare at another lady. "I beg your pardon, Miss Fairleigh."

She took his sincere apology as a request for clarification. "You like Miss Fernhill. I am glad. She is the nicest lady at the house party."

"I am sorry," he clarified. "I should have been paying my attention to you."

Miss Fairleigh gave the tiniest of shrugs. "I do not mind, Lord Hythe. She likes you, too. I have seen the way she looks at you."

"Do you really think so?" Hythe asked before he could trap the words behind his teeth.

"Oh yes," Miss Fairleigh insisted. "Not just because you are a really good catch, either. She enjoys talking to you. I can tell." She began counting points off on her fingers. "You are really clever, and she is really clever. You are kind and she is kind. You play chess and she plays chess. You enjoy tidying things, and she enjoys tidying things. You like to talk about government and machines and books, and she likes to talk about government and machines and books."

Hythe took her pause to think of some other connection between him and Miss Fernhill as the opportunity to interrupt. "Quite so, Miss Fairleigh." Far more insightful than he suspected. Miss Fairleigh might not have a sparkling intellect, but she possessed a lot of common sense.

"There is someone for everyone," Miss Fairleigh intoned. She frowned. "Except that Mr. Stone says marriage is not for everybody, and the two things cannot both be true, can they?"

Talking to Miss Fairleigh was somewhat like sinking into a deep feather pillow. The temptation to sleep was nearly irresistible. "Who is Mr. Stone, Miss Fairleigh?" Hythe asked, idly, more for something to say than out of interest.

Miss Fairleigh blushed. Hythe's attention sharpened. "Mr. Gerard Stone. A neighbour of my family in Sussex," she admitted. "May I tell you something in confidence, Lord Hythe?"

Hythe could not find the right words to persuade her to keep her secrets in time to stop her. "Gerard is my someone. Mama would like me to make a good match. She means someone with a title, but Gerard has land and comes from a good family. Papa said I must attend the parties Mama planned for me, and be pleasant to the gentlemen. He said if I did not find my affections engaged by someone else, I could go home for Christmas, and he would give his consent."

She beamed, suddenly beautiful in her joy. "This is the last party, Lord Hythe, and no one is better than Gerard. Not for me."

Hythe could help but smile back at her. She was a sweet young lady.

"Please do not smile at me like that, Lord Hythe," she scolded him. "I do not want Mama thinking you might like me."

Hythe told her the truth. "I do like you, Miss Fairleigh. I wish you and Mr. Stone every happiness."

Hythe did not linger with the gentlemen over the port, but by the time he reached the drawing room, Miss Fernhill was nowhere to be seen. He asked Lady Osbourne, trying to sound casual.

"In the light of tomorrow's travel, Lord Hythe, Lady Barker thought it best to retire early," Lady Osbourne told him.

"Of course," Hythe answered. Perhaps Miss Fernhill had changed her mind. Perhaps she had no real interest in him after all, whatever Miss Fairleigh thought.

One of the other young ladies asked if he would turn the pages for her while she played the piano. Hythe apologised and went up to bed himself.

CHAPTER NINE

"Pritchard," Hythe said, "I wish to get a note to a young lady, but I do not wish anyone else to find out."

In the mirror, he could see his valet pause over the trousers he was folding. "In the morning, my lord?" Pritchard asked, his face carefully blank.

Hythe sighed. "I suppose you are right. I feel this sense of urgency, as if she is going to leave early tomorrow, and I will not see her again. There was something wrong this evening, but she arrived late to dinner, and we were not seated together. How can I fix whatever is wrong if I do not know what it is?"

He was rambling. This was not Pritchard's problem. "I beg your pardon, Pritchard. I should not have asked."

Pritchard was frowning. "Might we be speaking of Miss Fernhill, my lord?"

Hythe turned on the dressing stool so he could see Pritchard face to face. "Do you know something, Pritchard?"

"There has been considerable upset downstairs, sir. After our own trouble this morning, a certain young person whom I will not call a lady and her mother were invited to leave. When Miss Fernhill and Lady Barker went up to their room before dinner, they found their belongings disturbed, many things destroyed, and noxious substances introduced to their bedding, my lord."

"Good Lord!" No wonder his poor love had looked so distressed. "You believe this was done by Miss Turnbull?"

Pritchard nodded. "The butler and housekeeper have been questioning the servants who were in that wing this afternoon. Miss Turnbull was seen by several different maids carrying chamber pots, and at least one maid saw her entering Miss Fernhill's room."

"That is conclusive," Hythe said. "She had no place in that room, and I doubt she has ever done a domestic chore in her life."

Pritchard returned to his folding. "I might add, my lord, that Lady Osbourne moved Miss Fernhill and Lady Barker to the rooms previously occupied by the Turnbull ladies. Their own room was uninhabitable. They are in the first two rooms on the left in the ladies' wing, my lord. First, Lady Barker, and then Miss Fernhill. Should you wish to slide a note under the door, my lord."

Enter the ladies' wing, and slide a note under a door? It was the sort of thing Hythe's new brother-in-law might once have done, or the Duke of Haverford back when he was a wild young man. Hythe had never indulged in such indiscretions. He found it impossible to forget that every lady was somebody's daughter and usually somebody's sister.

On the other hand, his intentions were honourable, and he

could not bear to let Miss Fernhill go without at least having her agree to visit him.

Pritchard had finished packing away Hythe's clothes, leaving out what he would wear to travel tomorrow. He picked up the bucket with the waste wash water and paused. "You may wish to know, my lord, that Miss Fernhill sent down for a posset after she and Lady Barker went up to bed. Apparently, Lady Barker has a sick headache."

He turned towards the door, and then back again to face Hythe. "Miss Fernhill is highly regarded in the Servants Hall, my lord. She always behaves in a ladylike manner even when no one is there but the servants, she is always courteous, and—I might add, my lord— very tidy in her room and her person." He bowed. "I will wish you a good night, sir."

That was a very strong recommendation from Hythe's exacting valet, particularly since Pritchard made it a point of pride to never state an opinion on anything Hythe chose to do or anyone with whom he spent time. The valet had a thousand silent ways to communicate disapproval. It seemed, however, that Miss Fernhill had Pritchard's unqualified support.

"Good night, Pritchard. And thank you."

Left to himself, Hythe stared at the banked fire and thought about creeping through the house after everyone else was asleep to deliver a note. It was a ridiculous idea. He was the Earl of Hythe. He didn't do that sort of thing. He could not stop thinking about it.

Rilla sat on the window seat in her new room. Through the glass, she could see little but grey on grey—dark shapes against a dark sky. Still, the only other chair was hard and uncomfortable. This room was smaller than the one she had shared with Cousin Felicia. On the other hand, it was one of a suite of two rooms, linked by an adjoining door, so Rilla had her bed to herself.

She had put Cousin Felicia into her maid's hands, to be changed for bed and fed a posset with a heavy dose of laudanum. Then she had come through the adjoining door to her own room, thinking to have an early night.

Instead, she had tossed and turned and eventually untangled herself from the bed clothes, wrapped herself in a blanket and retreated to the window.

Her thoughts were a muddle. Some of them were about the invasion of her room. She had never been the target of such personal malice. Even the baron, even her uncle, merely discounted her happiness and wellbeing as irrelevant to their own goals. They had not hated her.

Then there was the situation with Lord Hythe. Would she be able to talk to him in the morning? Would he reject her after he knew the truth about where she had been? Did she even want to be his countess, always in the public view, always required to be on stage and perfectly dressed and behaved?

What would his sisters think of her? One was the Countess of Sutton, wife to the heir to a duke. The other had been Hythe's hostess for years, both at diplomatic postings and at political dinners. Surely, they would not approve of Rilla, with her scandalous past, for their brother?

And yet, Hythe had spoken with approval of the Pilkingtons. He had said the missing years of her past could be managed. He implied he did not care.

On the other hand, Society had others like Miss Turnbull, who would hate her because she refused to be oppressed. Would marrying Lord Hythe mean spending the rest of her life with a target on her back?

He was a powerful man, with connections throughout the upper ton. He would be able to protect her. But would he want to marry her when he knew the truth?

The outer door squeaked slightly as it opened. Rilla froze. No one should be coming into her room at this time of night. Her first thought was that Miss Turnbull had returned, and her heart jolted at the possibility of an outright physical attack.

The shape crossing to the bed was too large to be Miss Turnbull, and the voice that called softly was male. "Veronica? Veronica, are you awake?"

Veronica was Miss Turnbull's name. This, then, was an assignation. Or was it an assault? And what should Rilla do? Stay silent and hope he left?

Before she could decide, the man bent to put a spill to the fire, and went round the room lighting candles. "Veronica, darling. Surprise!" It was Mr. Smythe, leaning over the bed and discovering it was empty.

Rilla could not have been more than a dark shape against the window, but he suddenly started towards her. "There you are."

"Miss Turnbull has left the house party," Rilla told him, warding him off with one hand while the other clutched the blankets.

"Has she?" he asked, with little interest. "Who have we here? Miss Fernhill!" In the candle-light, his teeth flashed white. "You will do."

"Please leave," Rilla told him, doing her best to sound calm and commanding. The words came out with a quaver. She really was a terrible actress.

He caught the wrist of the hand she held out to stop him, and stepped closer. "If you scream, the whole house will know you have had a man in your room. I have come here for a tup, Miss Fernhill, and a tup I will have. Give me a good ride, and I will tell nobody. How is that for a bargain?"

Rilla began to struggle in earnest, but he was too strong.

And then he was gone, ripped backwards by a forceful arm. It was Hythe, kneeling over the cad now, laying punch after punch into the man's face.

Hythe never lost his temper. Anger destroyed the ability to think logically and coherently, and how could one solve problems without clear thinking?

As he did his best to turn Smythe's face into pulp, he was in a blinding rage. Somewhere, dimly, he knew part of the rage was at himself. He had seen the swine slip into Miss Fernhill's room, and his first impulse had been to rush to the rescue. A doubt about her innocence had him stopping to observe.

He was a cad. He had told her, in essence, that he trusted her, and failed at the first test.

By the time Smythe's own words made it clear he was there for Miss Turnbull, Hythe had decided to keep his own presence secret, for Miss Fernhill's sake. Smythe would realise his mistake and go away without realising Hythe was in the vicinity. He would keep his own excursion quiet and would not know about Hythe's.

Then the dirty fiend made his attempt at blackmail and even dared to put his hands on Hythe's lady, and Hythe saw red.

Lost in the rhythm of his own blows, he was not aware that Smythe had stopped struggling, but Miss Fernhill's gentle voice and her touch on his shoulder brought him back to himself. "Lord Hythe. Lord Hythe."

He stood, dropping Smythe's collar. "I beg your pardon, Miss Fernhill. You should not have been subjected to that display."

Smythe groaned.

"Thank you for saving me," she replied. "I thought he was going to…" she shuddered.

Hythe fought back the urge to put his arms around her. "He can't be found here. Let me drag him out of this wing and call a footman to deal with him."

He could not just walk away and leave her. Not after such an experience. Not with so much unresolved between them.

"Will you and Lady Barker be able to meet me in the library in fifteen minutes?" he asked. "We need to talk."

Miss Fernhill nodded, and Hythe grabbed Smythe under his arms and dragged him from the room.

CHAPTER TEN

Which proves, say some, that the invaders were human. Surely supernatural beings would have used magic, not branches? But others scoff, and point to the fact that Miss Amaryllis Fernhill disappeared without a trace. Some say she suddenly reappeared in London, three years to the day after her disappearance. But whether she spent those years in heaven or hell or the land of Fairie, she would never say.

["The Abduction of Amaryllis Fernhill", in *Collected Tales from the Villages of England*, by a Gentleman]

Rilla should have told Lord Hythe that Lady Barker was dosed with laudanum and unlikely to wake until noon. She was going, even so. If he would not see her without a chaperone, then they would just have to make another time.

Or perhaps he would tell her he had turned his attention elsewhere. After all, most people would believe she must have given

Smythe some indication his assault would be welcomed. And then to go to the library on her own—he might feel justified in believing she was a harlot. Especially when she told him her story.

She was still going to go. She dressed in a day gown that buttoned up the front, one of the few gowns to escape destruction, wrapped herself in a shawl, and took a candle to light her way through the house.

The trip down to the library was a nightmare. The experience with Mr. Smythe had her shying at shadows and flinching with every creak and groan of the old house. By the time she was halfway there, she was trembling with panic. Retracing her steps seemed scarier than continuing, or she would have fled back to the defiled sanctuary of her room.

It was not until she was opening the library door that it occurred to her Lord Hythe might not be waiting. What if some other man was lurking within? What if he, like Mr. Smythe, took her presence alone as an invitation?

She peered around the door, and sobbed with relief as she recognised Lord Hythe, standing by the chess board over which they had spent so much time in this week.

He turned at the sound, smiled a greeting, and held out his arms as she ran to him and threw herself onto his chest. As he wrapped her in his embrace, she gave vent to her feelings in a gush of tears. Lord Hythe held her close, patting her back and murmuring comforting words, such as, "You are safe now. I have you. There, there, dear heart."

The release of fear and anguish gave way to a flood of embarrassment, and she lifted her head. "I must apologise. I have made your shoulder all wet."

He kept his arms around her, though he loosened them enough to allow her to lean back. "You have had a trying day," he said.

The understatement made her laugh. "You could say that."

He smiled in response, and kissed her nose. "My sisters assure me that a good cry helps them feel better."

"I never cry," Rilla told him.

He looked over her shoulder. "Is Lady Barker coming?"

Rilla bit her lip. Lord Hythe's eyes widened and darkened as they fixed on her mouth. "She took laudanum for her headache," Rilla explained.

Lord Hythe blinked and his gaze moved back up to her eyes. "In that case, my dear, please take a seat. I do not think I should be holding you in my arms without a chaperone nearby."

"I trust you," Rilla assured him, but she took the hand he offered her and allowed him to see her to a chair.

Lord Hythe's smile was a little strained. "Thank you. I shall endeavour to be worthy of your trust."

"You are," Miss Fernhill assured him, fervently, which confirmed she knew little about men and their passions. Having lost control of his emotions in her room, he now held them on a very fragile tether.

He'd heard soldiers speak about the way the urge to kill transmuted after a battle into an urge to—as it were—celebrate life in a primal fashion. He now understood that impulse from the inside, the leftover emotions from rearranging Smythe's face making the desire he always felt for Miss Fernhill a primitive force that tore at his restraint.

He took a seat on the other side of the chess board. She bit her lip again, which wasn't making him any more comfortable. He took a deep breath.

"Did Smythe hurt you?" he suddenly thought to ask, berating himself for not thinking of it earlier.

"My wrist, a little. You arrived before he did more. He thought the room was still..."

Hythe reached for her wrist. It was not swollen. Nor, in the candle light, did it look bruised. "Miss Turnbull's. Yes. I heard what he said to you, the hound."

"It is why... That is, I never cry. But Smythe's attack, coming after Miss Turnbull's. And then the walk down to the library. It was foolish. I knew in my head no one was about to leap out on me, but my heart did not believe my head. By the time I arrived here, I was so frightened… I have never been more pleased to see a person than half an hour ago in my bedroom and just before, here in the library."

She had left her hand resting in his. He traced patterns on it with his thumbs. Whatever she had been doing during her absence from Society, it had not made calluses, though the hands were firmer and more muscular than those of a typical indolent Society maiden.

She took a breath with a bit of a shudder, as if suppressing tears, but her voice was even when she spoke. "I came to tell you my story, my lord. If, afterwards, you wish to withdraw your offer, I will understand."

Hythe nodded, not bothering to tell her that Smythe's attack made it essential for them to marry. Two men had been in her bedchamber, and one of them could not be trusted to keep his mouth shut. All Hythe's doubts about the wisdom of his course had been laid to rest. It was his duty to marry Miss Fernhill and save her reputation.

He might have been resigned to the necessity. Instead, he was exultant. The lovely Amaryllis Fernhill would be his wife, and neither her doubts nor his, nor the opinions of the rest of the Polite World, mattered a farthing.

Miss Fernhill began her story. "Perhaps you will guess when you know that Lady Emma Pilkington has been my best friend since we were both infants. We grew up on adjoining estates. She fell in love with a young army officer. However, her father would not entertain his suit, but instead attempted to betroth Emma to Alfred Hargreaves, the son of the baron next door to us both. He is a horrible man, who would have treated her terribly."

Hythe recognised the name Emma Pilkington and had an inkling of where this might be going. "And her preferred suitor was Joseph Pilkington, I take it. She eloped?"

Miss Fernhill was focusing on her hands, and on his thumbs, stroking her fingers over and over. "Yes, overseas with the army.

They married. Then Joseph received a small inheritance and Emma became enceinte. He sold out and they used his money to start a small acting troupe."

"Which came to your rescue when you needed them, and staged the heavenly rescue," he guessed.

She looked up, searched his face, and then returned his smile. "You do not mind?"

"I am grateful to them. You must introduce me when we are back in London so I can thank them." She had travelled with an acting troupe! That would take a bit of getting used to, and was likely to cause a scandal if it got out.

"I cannot act, of course, and—besides—I was anxious to stay out of sight, at least at first. So, I was their stage manager and wardrobe mistress. For two and a half years, until I was nearly twenty-five. Emma and Joseph had graduated to playing in theatres, and they took me to Cousin Felicia when they had an engagement in York. She knows everything, by the way. And now, so do you."

He lifted her fingers to his mouth for a kiss. "I do. And it is not such a great matter, is it? You had to hide from a forced marriage to a wicked brute. You took refuge with a married couple, one the daughter of an earl and the other the grandson of a marquis. You stayed in their protection until you were free of the guardianship of your larcenous uncle, and then your cousin sponsored your Season."

He was reasonably certain the clever ladies of his family could cast the situation in that positive light. Even if they could not, the scandal would blow over in time. It might slow his advancement in the House of Lords, but he was too useful a diplomat for that part of his career to be affected.

"Will you marry me, Amaryllis Fernhill?" he asked.

"I thought you wanted your sisters to meet me first," she protested.

"If you need more time before you give me an answer, I will wait," he agreed. "For my part, my heart is set on you, dear one. I admire you. I enjoy your conversation and your company. I desire you more than I care to discuss while you are still an innocent. I want to spend the rest of my life with you at my side, as my countess, my wife, and my friend. Do you need more time, Amaryllis?"

She blushed, but she did not avoid his eyes. "Are you certain? If you change your mind, you need only…"

"Trust me, dear one. I will not change my mind."

"Then, yes. If you think I would suit." She cast her eyes down then looked up through her lashes. "I admire you. I enjoy your conversation and your company. I want to spend the rest of my life with you at my side. And I am an innocent, as you say, but if desire is the burning need for your touch, and the conviction that you, and you alone can show me the mystery of why that should be…"

She got no further, because he had taken her mouth with his, leaning across the table and scattering chess pieces every which way.

EPILOGUE

Others argue that the rumours are untrue. Would a maiden who had spent three years in the Faerie Kingdom settle for a mere earl in faraway London? Amaryllis Fernhill never returned to Pluffington-on-Memmerbeck, and none of the villagers are ever likely to go to London, so every granny and each gaffer is free to hold their own opinion.

["The Abduction of Amaryllis Fernhill", in *Collected Tales from the Villages of England*, by a Gentleman]

The Earl of Hythe rolled his countess to her side, still within his embrace. "Good morning, Amaryllis Belvoir," he murmured, the same morning greeting he had given her the day after their wedding fifteen years ago, and repeated every day since.

Rilla gave him the same saucy answer she'd made fifteen years ago. "It has been good so far, Nathan Belvoir."

He kissed her again. "Every time," he told her, and it was true.

Physical intimacy with her husband had been wonderful from the beginning, and it just got better over the years.

They had married in London three weeks after the end of the house party—a small ceremony at St George's with a handful of witnesses. Cousin Felicia, the Pilkingtons, Hythe's sister Sophia and her husband James, and the Duke and Duchess of Winshire. The newly-weds spent Christmas at Belvoir Close. By the time they returned to Society in the Spring, the duchess and her friends had convinced Society that Rilla was a romantic heroine—the innocent victim of villainous plotting saved by the cleverness of a faithful friend, and now returned to her rightful place through the true love of one of Society's favourite sons.

Yesterday had been their wedding anniversary. They had been travelling, but still found the energy to celebrate in the time-honoured fashion. Twice. Last night before they slept and again this morning.

They lay for a while, enjoying the comfort of one another's arms and the warm blankets on this cold December morning. "We have to get up," Rilla said, with little conviction. There were probably warm embers under the banked fire and, elsewhere in the inn, the twins would be awake. Their younger sister, too, but she was probably still in bed with a book. The boys rose with the larks, bright eyed and ripe for mischief.

"Five more minutes," Hythe decreed, and Rilla snuggled closer.

"What do you want to do first?" Hythe asked, after a while.

They had detoured to Pluffington-on-Memmerbeck on a whim, and this morning, Rilla planned to show her family the places of her childhood. As she and Hythe put on the nightwear they only ever wore in the morning, in order not to scandalise his valet and her maid, they discussed where they would go. The church, the village shop, the cottages of the tenants she used to visit, the manor house where she lived, if they could gain access. The secret glade where she and Emma had plotted her escape.

The Pritchards arrived with hot washing water, morning chocolate for Rilla and coffee for Hythe, and the expected news that their daughter Lady Emma was awake but not yet up while Lord Martin and Master Richard were eating their breakfast in the inn's public dining room. "Andrews is keeping an eye on them," Pritchard assured the scoundrels' parents. Their head groom would make sure the boys did not step too far out of bounds.

Pritchard had also discovered that the distant cousin who inherited from Rilla's uncle was not in residence, but the housekeeper had permission to show interested visitors around the historic building. That would work. Rilla had no intention of letting the locals know she was the girl who once escaped from that house.

Breakfast was laid for Lord and Lady Hythe and their daughter in a private parlour. Within minutes they were joined by the two boys, who each filched a bun from the basket on the table and took a seat. Of course, they were still hungry after breaking their own fast with a full country spread. They were fourteen, and it was impossible to fill them.

"We have been listening to the local legend, Mama," Martin said.

Richard made an expansive flourish with his bun. "Miss Amaryllis Fernhill, carried off by angels."

"Or devils. Or faeries. I am looking forward to seeing the church where everything happened." Martin grinned. "It was a very exciting story. I particularly enjoyed the end!"

"You are wrong, Martin," his father said. "The abduction of Miss Amaryllis Fernhill was only the beginning."

But as for the young romantics of the village, they believe the lady is still in the other realm, the consort of the Faerie King, where she will live happily ever after. And why not? It is as good an end to the story as any other.

["The Abduction of Amaryllis Fernhill", in *Collected Tales from the Villages of England*, by a Gentleman]

ABOUT JUDE KNIGHT

Jude always wanted to be a novelist. She started in her teens, but life kept getting in the way. Years passed, and with them dozens of unfinished manuscripts. The fear grew. What if she tried, failed, and lost the dream forever? The years since 2014 have brought 15 novels and counting, 16 novella, 5 volumes of short stories, 3 awards, and hundreds of positive reviews. The dream is alive.

Website and blog: http://judeknightauthor.com/

Subscribe to newsletter: http://judeknightauthor.com/newsletter/

Bookshop: https://shop.judeknightauthor.com/

Facebook: https://www.facebook.com/JudeKnightAuthor/

Bookbub: https://www.bookbub.com/profile/jude-knight

REGENCY BOOKS BY JUDE KNIGHT

Fairy tales reinterpreted (loosely) as Regency romances, but with magical elements transformed into natural happenings and the role of hero and heroine reversed.

Lady Beast's Bridegroom (Book 1 in *A Twist Upon a Regency Tale*)

Is the love of Beauty and his Lady Beast strong enough to overcome prejudice, hatred, and rejection?

The Talons of a Lyon (Part of the Lyon's Den Connected World)

Lance promised Mrs Dove Lyon he would take Lady Frogmore from Pond Street into High Society. Her nasty relatives are determined he will fail.

PUBLISHED APRIL 2023

One Perfect Dance (Book 2 in *A Twist Upon a Regency Tale*)

For sixteen years, Ash has owed Regina a dance. His step-brothers will do anything to keep him from the ball.

Published May 2023

Also in this series, *Snowy and the Seven Doves* (august 2023) and *Perchance to dream* (November 2023)

THE GOLDEN REDEPENNINGS SERIES

True love is rare and elusive, but they won't settle for less

Candle's Christmas Chair (A novella in *The Golden Redepennings* series)

They are separated by social standing and malicious lies. He has until Christmas to convince her to give their love another chance.

Gingerbread Bride (A novella in *The Golden Redepennings* series)

Mary runs from an unwanted marriage and finds adventure, danger and her girlhood hero, coming once more to her rescue.

Farewell to Kindness (Book 1 in *The Golden Redepennings* series)

Love is not always convenient. Anne and Rede have different goals, but when their enemies join forces, so must they.

A Raging Madness (Book 2 in *The Golden Redepennings* series)

Their marriage is a fiction. Their enemies are all too real. Uncovering the truth will need all the trust Ella and Alex can find.

The Realm of Silence (Book 3 in *The Golden Redepennings* series)

Rescue her daughter, destroy her dragons, defeat his demons, return to his lonely life. How hard can it be?

Unkept Promises (Book 4 in *The Golden Redepennings* series)

Mia hopes to negotiate a comfortable marriage. Jules wants his wife to return to England, where she belongs. Love confounds them both.

The Flavour of Our Deeds (Book 5 in The Golden Redepenning series)

When Luke finally admits to loving Kitty, she thinks their troubles are over. They are just beginning.

Published in March 2023

The Golden Redepennings: Books 1 to 4

The first four books of the series are now available in box set form:

THE RETURN OF THE MOUNTAIN KING

In 1812, high Society is rocked when the heir to the Duke of Winshire, long thought dead, returns to England with

the children of his Persian-born wife and fierce armed retainers.

To Wed a Proper Lady: The Bluestocking and the Barbarian (Book 1 in The Return of the Mountain King series)

Everyone knows James needs a bride with impeccable blood lines. He needs Sophia's love more.

To Mend the Broken-Hearted: The Healer and the Hermit (Book 2 in The Return of the Mountain King series)

A woman doctor from a foreign land and a recluse earl with a missing hand find common ground nursing the children he loves, whether they are his or not.

Melting Matilda (A novella in the Return of the Mountain King series)

Sparks flew a year ago when the Granite Earl kissed the Ice Princess. In the depths of another winter, fire still smoulders under the frost between them.

To Claim the Long-Lost Lover: The Diamond and the Doctor (Book 3 in The Return of the Mountain King series)

The beauty known as the Winderfield Diamond hides a ruinous secret. Society's newest viscount holds the key.

To Tame the Wild Rake: The Saint and the Sinner (Book 4 in The Return of the Mountain King series)

The whole world knows Aldridge is a wicked sinner. The ton has labelled Charlotte a saint for her virtue and good works. Appearances can be deceptive.

Paradise Triptych (A collection in The Return of the Mountain King series)

Long ago, when they were young, James and Eleanor were deeply in love. But their families tore them apart and they went on to marry other people. This set of two novellas and a set of memoirs tells their story.

LION'S ZOO

New series starting in June 2023, as officers from an elite cadre of exploring officers return to England and find love and danger.

Chaos Come Again, PUBLICATION IN JUNE 2023

Grasp the Thorn, PUBLICATION IN JULY 2023

OTHER NOVELS

A Baron for Becky

She was a fallen woman. How could the men who loved her help set her back on her feet?

Revealed in Mist

As spy and enquiry agent, Prue and David worked to uncover secrets, while hiding a few of their own.

House of Thorns

His rose thief bride comes with a scandal that threatens to tear them apart.

OTHER NOVELLAS

The Husband Gamble [This novella]

When the pawn becomes Queen, she and the opposing King will both win the game of love.

Lord Calne's Christmas Ruby

One wealthy merchant's heiress with an aversion to fortune hunters. One an impoverished earl with a twisted hand. Combine and stir with one villainous rector.

A Suitable Husband

A chef from the slums, however talented, is no fit mate for the cousin of a duke, however distant. But Cedrica can dream.

The Beast Next Door (A novella in the Bluestocking Belles collection *Valentines from Bath*)

In all the assemblies and parties, no-one Charis met could ever match the beast next door.

A Dream Come True (A novella in the Bluestocking Belles collection Storm & Shelter)

The tempest that batters Barnaby Somerville's village is the latest but not the least of his challenges. He does not expect the storm that will batter his heart.

Lord Cuckoo Comes Home (A novella in the Bluestocking Belles collection *Desperate Daughters*)

Two people who have never fitted in just might be a perfect fit.

LUNCH-LENGTH READS: STORY COLLECTIONS

Hand-Turned Tales and Lost in the Tale

A double handful of short stories and novellas, free from most eretailers. Try the range of Jude's imagination one bite at a time, in a lunch-length read.

If Mistletoe Could Tell Tales

A repackaging of six published Christmas stories: four novellas and two novelettes. Because nothing enhances the magic of Christmas like the magic of love.

Hearts in the Land of Ferns

Five stories all set in New Zealand: two historical and three contemporary suspense. All That Glisters has been published in Hand-Turned Tales. The other four have all been published in multi-author collections, but never before in a collection of Jude Knight stories.

Chasing the Tale and Chasing the Tale: Volume 11

Short stories just long enough for a lunch or coffee break. In volume 1: Nine Regency plus one colonial New Zealand and one medieval Scotland. In volume 2: mostly Regency, with one Victorian New Zealand. Multiple tropes, catastrophes and barriers on the way to a happy ending.

CPSIA information can be obtained
at www.ICGtesting.com
Printed in the USA
LVHW100951110323
741369LV00002B/82

9 781991 199614